HARE'S CHOICE

Hare's Choice

BY *Dennis Hamley*

ILLUSTRATED BY

MEG RUTHERFORD

Delacorte Press

Published by
Delacorte Press
Bantam Doubleday Dell Publishing Group, Inc.
666 Fifth Avenue
New York, New York 10103

Illustrations are executed in watercolor wash.

This work was first published in
Great Britain by Andre Deutsch Limited.

Library of Congress Cataloging in Publication Data

Hamley, Dennis.
Hare's choice / by Dennis Hamley; illustrated by Meg Rutherford.
p.   cm.
Summary: A hare killed by a car is found by two children
who take it to school where they and their classmates write a
story about it—giving it a choice to make in the afterworld.
ISBN 0-385-30050-6
[1. Hares—Fiction.   2. Death—Fiction.   3. Storytelling—Fiction.
4. Schools—Fiction.]   I. Rutherford, Meg, ill.   II. Title.
PZ7.H18294Har   1990
[Fic]—dc20   89-36857   CIP   AC

Manufactured in the United States of America
Designed by Jane Byers Bierhorst
April 1990
10 9 8 7 6 5 4 3 2 1
FFG

FOR ALL THE CHILDREN
IN WRITING COURSES EVERYWHERE

For, don't you mark? we're made so that we love
First when we see them painted, things we have passed
Perhaps a hundred times nor cared to see;
And so they are better, painted—better to us,
Which is the same thing.

From "Fra Lippo Lippi"
by Robert Browning

Contents

Hare

A clear, starry night with a low moon. The day, when it came, would be fine and warm. Now it was cold on the open down. Far below, the road stretched dark into the village. The hedges that had once lined it had long since been uprooted. Now it snaked across miles of openness except where it was hidden by low patches of mist. Above, a grove of trees crowned the horizon, black on the moon-lit gray of the grass. The creatures of the night moved through its trees and out into the open. The language of the night chattered, rustled, screamed, and hooted. Thousands of short, intense lives started, continued, and ended.

Out on the down but only fifty yards from the edge of the grove, the hares fed. Twelve of them; they munched the new spring grass as if tomorrow none would be left. Huge lumps of unchewed greenery passed down their gullets for their digestive systems to deal with later. Mushrooms, puffballs, anything they found, went the same way. They ate: then they rested. All the time they listened, long ears twitching. What might surprise them, coming sudden out of the dark wood?

At precisely the same instant they all stopped eating. They rose up on their hind legs, attentive. Nothing. The pulse of danger all had felt at once died. The does ate on, unconcerned, five sets of long teeth ripping the grass. For the seven bucks, eating was finished. They sat in a wide circle, watching each other intently. Without warning, one bounded into the middle of the circle: another met him

and they sparred wildly. Suddenly, all was bewildering action. The others sprang into movement; they stood on their hind legs; they ran around in tight, furious circles; they started aimless cuffing fights that ceased as abruptly.

The does continued eating. Knowing what the bucks were up to, they were not interested in the ritual—only its outcome. The fighting, the running, the gamboling, carried on with silent concentration. Yet it never left the area of the first circle.

The moon was fading. Streaks of dawn showed to the east on this fine May morning. The grass showed first hints of color. The bucks still sported; the does still ate.

Then again that pulse of danger. The hares froze where they were with ears, nostrils, and eyes taking in messages. Was the danger from the wood, from the sky, or down in the valley where the humans were? It didn't matter where. Danger was near.

At the same instant every hare bolted, each his or her own way. The one message had reached them all—danger was coming out of the wood. The hares' forms—the shallow little homes they had made—lay in many different directions. Each hare now said, "I am the only one of my kind in the world; where I go is my business alone." Some made for their forms: others, once running, kept on. One such was the biggest and sleekest of the does. She ran down the slope, toward the road. Soon she had left the others way behind. She was not heading for her form or the forms where each of the leverets in her last litter had been placed. They were on their own now; three months old and fending for themselves. She was solitary. She owed nothing to buck, leveret, anyone. This was how she should be. This is how hares are.

Running downhill was hard work. The strong, muscled hind legs were too big for the short front legs and she longed for the level ground or the chance of an upward

slope. But above—that was where the danger lay; fox slinking out of the wood, man guarding his trees from long hare teeth. Whatever it was, she would not change direction yet.

So she ran at an angle down the hill to minimize the slope. And morning light greened the grass still further and the village far along the road made its first stirrings.

She reached the valley floor. Now the ground was more level. The message of danger was gone. The sheer joy of running flooded her; push with mighty hind legs, bound with springy front legs—push, bound, push, bound, push, bound . . . well into the unprotected openness of the hedgeless ground above the road.

Then, filtering into her brain again, the pulse of danger. Where? Was it the same danger back again? Was it a new one from a completely different source?

She stopped. Up on back legs, ears stretched, nostrils wrinkling.

Above. Something was above. In the sky was something strong, deadly, and faster even than she was, ready to swoop. She could not imagine this thing but she knew in the depths of her brain that it was there and that it meant death.

She doubled back, uphill. Now her hind legs took on an even faster rhythm and her front legs needed hardly to do more than balance her. She turned suddenly, then zig-zagged back toward the grove. Always she knew of the hooded eyes far above, watching every move she made like brown stitching in green cloth.

Ahead grazed sheep with their spring lambs. Now she made straight for them; her brain knew that the attack must come before she reached safe shelter with the flock.

And here it was; a whistling, snarling whirring through the air; a living thunderbolt. She turned and faced the hawk's talons, hooked beak, and the brown spreading

feathers. She was ready; whiplash kicks with the clawed back legs, swipes with the clawed forelegs. She was bigger than the bird. But was she stronger? And she had no stiletto-pointed beak and though her claws could draw blood she kept them short by scratching wood because they were not needed for killing.

Hawk and hare closed with each other; rolled over on the ground. She buffeted the hawk so the beak and talons kept away from her. Time and again the hawk's beak lunged, the talons raked. But the hare kicked ferociously and suffered no more than the sudden pain of light scratches down her flanks.

The hawk stood off; she knew it would come again before she reached the sheep. It did; they fought once more—kicks, cuffs, and archings of the supple body against beak, talons, and beating wings. But she sensed the hawk was weakening and, though she was now weak as well, knew safety was near. She summoned her strength for one last kick. She caught the bird a glancing blow and it made off to perch exhausted in a tree at the edge of the grove: to reconsider.

At last she reached the sheep and flopped down, dead beat, among them. They cropped the grass unconcerned as her strength came back and she bit at the long scratches that were all the hawk had left on her.

The sun rose higher. She was strong again. The danger, she knew, was done; the hawk was after easier prey. The cuts smarted but her brain was wiped clean of the struggle that had nearly been the end of her. The urge to run was on her again and she was away, awkwardly downhill.

The shock of her movement sent the sheep scattering, great white clouds over the green as the morning shadows spread. The sun was rising higher in a clear sky. She bounded on and reached the road. She stopped, surprised at the unfamiliar hardness under her pads. Before she moved again a new noise came and she rose on her hind legs to catch it. Her brain told her it was not the sort of danger she was used to. She looked one way, then another along the dark gray strip of road.

The noise came nearer; it was made by a vast beast, bright red, which was approaching at unimaginable speed. She felt no sense of danger. But a new feeling came as she watched the creature—sheer exhilaration. This red beast did not bound as other animals but seemed to roll on legs that were round. This new thing was powerful and fast. And so was she. A thrill of strength surged through her. They would run together, she and the red beast, to see who was the faster, the more powerful.

Before the red beast reached her she started running, daring it to catch her. She strained every muscle—push, bound, push, bound, push, bound. She was running faster than she had ever run before. But the red beast caught up with her. She looked at it as it drew level and forced herself to even greater speed.

And joy! the red beast did not pass. She was matching it for speed. Sheer pleasure in running with a beast worthy to pit herself against kept her going.

"John, slow down a minute. Look at this."

The woman was looking at the hare as it ran—brown, streamlined, and singleminded—beside the car.

The driver heard his wife and peered over at the side of the road.

"Good heavens," he said, and reduced speed so that the car and the hare ran neck and neck.

"It's beautiful," breathed the woman.

"I'll let it get ahead," said the man. "We'll look at it from all angles."

"I wish I had my camera," said the woman.

A beast that ran but did not hunt. A beast she could share the glory of speed with. The muscles in her hind legs bunched and loosened, bunched and loosened, driving her on. She turned her head in triumph toward the steep, shiny red sides of the beast. And—joy again!—the beast began to fall behind. She was winning. In ecstasy she began to tear around in great circles next to the road. As if acknowledging defeat the red beast stopped.

"If I hadn't seen this, I would never have believed it," said the man.

"A portable video camera. That's what I'd like right now," said the woman.

The hare stopped suddenly, rose on her hind legs, and looked at them steadily and unafraid. Then she shot away straight down the road, continuing her old course.

"Come on," said the man. "We'll follow her to the end."

The beast was friendly. It did not hunt and kill like a dog or a fox. It did not swoop from the air like a hawk. It raced her and then stopped to watch her. Perhaps it was like herself, needing no one and threatening no one.

She was once again running in a straight line along the road, daring the beast to catch her up. It did so very soon. Side by side they were, the beast always a little behind. Hare had won. Hare was the fast one. Hare was queen of the fields and the road. An urge to show off to this big, friendly, inferior beast came over her. She stopped running and began to leap and cavort, twisting her body in the air before she reached the ground.

The beast stopped again.

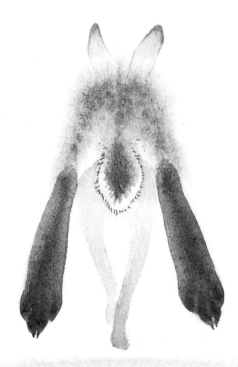

"It's marvelous," said the woman in wonder.

"We haven't got all day, you know," said the man.

Running again. Beast following. Tired now of straight lines. An urge to zigzag. In front of this friendly beast, which will follow as it always does. She changed course violently into the road—*Look at me! Look at me!*

Joy shone out of her bulging eyes.

The car was moving again. Hare galloped by its side. Suddenly she disappeared. There was a slight but audible bump at the front of the car. The driver braked hard.

"Oh, my God," he said.

The couple got out. Hare lay stretched in the road by the front left wheel. She was stone dead. The only wounds were scratches on her flanks where the blood was sticky.

"Those can't be anything to do with us," said the man.

"Why did the silly creature do that?" said the woman. "It was like suicide. Like a lemming."

"At least it was quick," said the man.

"We ought to bury it," said the woman. "We owe that to the creature."

"Be sensible," said the man. "Where am I going to get a spade from? Anyway, we've wasted enough time already."

"We can't leave it here," said the woman.

"And we can't take it with us," said the man. "I don't fancy jugged hare for my supper."

The woman looked at him with sudden distaste.

"I'm going to lay it out on the roadside grass properly," she said. Her voice gained a sarcastic edge. "Perhaps someone will find it who has a little time to spare."

She stooped, picked up the limp and surprisingly heavy form, and placed it gently on the grass. She looked at it silently for a moment; then she stooped again, picked two buttercups and a sprig of cow parsley, and laid them on each side of the furry brown body. She straightened and again looked down on it for a full minute while the man sat in the car drumming his fingers impatiently on the dashboard.

At length the woman reentered the car. Without looking at her the man restarted the engine and they were moving again. After a mile or so, when they had passed through the village, the man looked over toward his wife. Her face was blotched with silent tears and even as he looked she wiped them away with a tissue.

He turned away, looked straight ahead, and felt soiled. And the feeling did not leave him for many weeks.

Hare was in a black void. Other once-living creatures, millions upon millions of them, were with her—insects, birds, fish; animals from the tiniest marmoset to the hugest elephant. All released from the earth that day—some suddenly and violently, as Hare had been; some quietly and inevitably at the ends of their natural spans. In a black void together yet each one separate.

T W O

School

The sun rose higher in the blue morning sky. More cars, a truck or two, a school bus, passed by, leaving Hare still stretched by the road.

And now approached two figures, walking toward the village. A boy and a girl, each about ten. Harry and Sarah. They wore gray jerseys and blue jeans. They both had short brown hair and carried everything they needed for school in plastic shopping bags from supermarket checkouts. Twin brother and sister. From Spinney Farm, two miles out of the village. Coming to school in the old Victorian building next to the church, to meet twenty-five others and their two teachers.

They walked carefully, facing the traffic. The bare down rose shallowly around them. The landscape was familiar and seemed right to them. They were too young ever to have known the days when their walk would have been in the shade of thick hedges.

They didn't talk much as they walked. They knew each other too well for speech. But a mile from the village Sarah stopped.

"What's that?" she said. "On the other side of the road."

Harry stared over.

"Someone's run over a stray cat," he said.

"It's not. It's a big rabbit," said Sarah. "I'm going to have a look."

She crossed the road. Harry followed.

"It is," said Sarah. "It's a great big rabbit. Bigger than any I've ever seen before."

"Its colors are different from an old rabbit," said Harry.

They looked more carefully. The creature was not by any means brown all over. The back had tiny black dots all over it; as Sarah stroked the body, she realized the dots were made by tough, long black hairs amid the softer brown. The chest and stomach were white. The head and the back of the neck were a lighter brown while the face lower down merged almost into white. The legs, brown on the outside, became a deep gold inside.

"Look at its ears," said Sarah.

They were very long—longer even than those of any rabbit she had ever seen.

"And look at those back legs," said Harry. "I wouldn't want a kick from one of them."

They were indeed huge. No creature with legs like those would be content just to hop around outside a burrow.

"It's a hare," said Sarah.

"It's beautiful," said Harry. "And there's not a mark on it except those scratches on its side."

"What shall we do?" said Sarah. "We can't just leave it here."

"We ought to bury it," said Harry.

"A lovely thing like that should have a proper funeral," said Sarah. She looked at the ground again. "Someone's been here before. They left flowers. That's a message."

She picked up the wilting buttercups and cow parsley.

"Let's take it to school," said Harry.

"There's blood on it," said Sarah. "All sticky where it's been scratched."

"You're not afraid of a bit of blood, are you?" said Harry.

"Of course I'm not," said Sarah. "I just don't want it all over my clothes. Anyway, it'll have fleas."

"So you don't want to take it to school," said Harry.

"Yes, I do," said Sarah. "We need something to wrap it in."

She thought for a moment, then said, "Put all your stuff in my plastic bag. Then we can wrap her up in yours."

Harry did so, then ripped his bag down the sides so it made one long sheet of plastic. Now the hare could be carried easily without touching clothes or skin.

"It's heavier than you'd think," Harry said.

They took it in turns to cradle the creature in their arms as they finished their journey to school.

Neither Mr. Bray nor Mrs. Hoskins objected to a dead animal rapidly going stiff being brought into their school. They were always on the lookout for new objects of interest. And the pupils were eager to bring them. Funny-looking carrots and potatoes of the sort that usually get sent to "Ripley's Believe It or Not"; birds' eggs which (Mr. Bray was assured by kids with wide-eyed frankness) had fallen out of nests and smashed; on one occasion Jimmy Craddock, now at the secondary school in town, had brought in a complete wasps' nest. After three years it was still on display, like an antique football. So a dead hare held no fears. After all, Mr. Bray reasoned, country children see death around them all the time.

"As long as we bury it before school's out," he said. "Harry, I think that should be your responsibility."

There were only two classes in the school—the infant class was for children from six to eight, and the junior class was for nine- to eleven-year-olds. Mr. Bray and Mrs. Hoskins made sure they saw both regularly. And both teachers were interested in the hare. So while Mrs. Hoskins took the infants, Mr. Bray talked to the juniors with the hare stretched out on a cloth on the table in front of him. He told them all about the hare; how it was a mysterious animal and once was sacred. How it kept itself solitary, how it ran and leapt and gamboled and always did unexpected things. How it was different from the rabbit; how its lip was split in a different way; how its heart in relation to its body was huge and propelled vast amounts of blood through its veins so it could run fast over great distances. How the hare used to be called "Puss" and a few people had kept them as pets. How the hare's behavior made people think it was mad, so it was associated with the moon, with tricks and pranks, and—for a time—as much with witches as cats were.

"It's a wonderful and strange animal," said Mr. Bray. "And I'm sorry this one's dead, but it's a rare privilege to see such a superb specimen as this doe so close."

Sarah stroked the brown head again. The animal was getting stiff now and she felt somehow as if she had to do something before it slipped away from her entirely. In five and a half hours' time Harry had to bury it.

"Poor puss," she said. And then—"I want to write a story about her."

She couldn't quite explain this sudden feeling. But somehow she knew that if she could do this the hare would stay alive for her even after Harry had shoveled the dark earth on top of the body.

"So do I," said Harry unexpectedly.

He felt the same. Burying the hare would be the end. And as they had taken turns to carry it along the road, both had known in the instinctive way twins have that this lovely animal even in death meant a lot to them.

Sarah looked at him gratefully.

"Can we?" she said to Mr. Bray. "Before school ends?"

Mrs. Hoskins had come in to join Mr. Bray.

"Do you want to write one together?" she said. "Or separately?"

"I want to write my own," said Harry. "I've got an idea already."

Sarah looked disappointed.

"I wanted to talk about it first with other people," she said. "I don't want to just start writing."

"Perhaps everybody should have a go at this," said Mr. Bray.

A murmur of agreement ran around the room.

"Why not get into two groups?" said Mrs. Hoskins. "Sarah leads one and Harry the other. Then you can talk the stories through and perhaps we'll get some first drafts by the end of the day."

Harry wasn't too keen on this idea.

"Who's thinking of coming in my group, then?" he said truculently. He was warning people off.

"What's the idea you've had, Harry?" said Mr. Bray. "If people know that, they'll know whether they want to join you or not."

"Well," said Harry unwillingly, "there's been this great nuclear holocaust, you see. And everything's been wiped out. All living things. Except the hares. Because they were immune to radioactivity and all that."

"How?" said a suspicious boy whose name was Tim.

"I don't know," said Harry irritably. "They just were, that's all. They'd always been immune, only no scientists had ever noticed."

"Why not?" said Tim.

"Because they never bothered to look, that's why," said Harry. "Anyway, there's only hares left in the world. And she here"—pointing to the dead hare—"she's their leader. She's like that queen when the Romans were here. What's her name?"

"Boadicea?" suggested Mr. Bray.

"That's the one," said Harry. "And that's what they call this hare. Now they're the only ones left on earth, these hares have learned to read and all stuff like that. Anyway, there's this extraterrestrial invasion; this whole crowd from another galaxy has found out there's a whole world here with only hares on it, so they invade. And Boadicea here, she leads the hares in a great last battle. By now they've invented guns and rockets and tanks and things."

"Who have? The hares?" Tim's voice was derisive.

"Of course. Dead easy for them now they're the only ones left. So there's this great battle and the hares kill all the extraterrestrials and destroy their spaceships with laser beams. But just as the hares win their final victory, Boadicea is killed."

"How?" said Tim, still the persistent interlocutor.

"I don't know," said Harry. Then inspiration struck. "Nobody knows. She was just like we found her. Unmarked. Except for scratches on her sides."

"Ah," said Tim, this time with an expression of great satisfaction. "Germ warfare. The extraterrestrials infected the open wounds. That was a cunning trick, to try it on the Queen Hare first. They hope that the hares will be too fed up to look for an antidote now their leader's dead. But the hares will have to, otherwise they'll all die themselves and the extraterrestrial survivors will take over because they're immune to diseases on earth. But the spirit of the Queen lives on and the hares don't give in. They work all night and find the antidote and so the extraterrestrials are finished after all."

Harry looked at Tim with admiration. Suddenly sharing didn't seem so bad.

"That's brilliant," he said.

"Well," said Mr. Bray, "we've all heard Harry's story and how discussion can change things. What lines are your thoughts taking you on, Sarah?"

"I keep thinking about what you said about hares being the familiars of witches, like cats," said Sarah. "I'd like to write something about witches."

"All right," said Mr. Bray. "We've got Harry's extraterrestrials and Sarah's witches. Can we get more or less equal groups out of that choice?"

Indeed they could. And it was by no means all boys on one side, all girls on the other. With Harry there were four other boys, including Tim, and two girls; with Sarah four girls and three boys. So the fifteen-strong junior class had divided itself fairly neatly.

Sarah's group got down to business quickly.

"What about my witch idea, then?" said Sarah.

"I don't think a hare would be a witch's familiar, like a cat," said Emma.

Sarah looked annoyed.

"Why did you come in my group, then?" she said.

"I thought we were going to discuss it," said Emma.

"I think it *could* be a sort of familiar," said Roy. "But it wouldn't be *quite* the same. A cat stays with you all the time but a hare keeps taking off."

"Perhaps the devil comes to the witch in the shape of a hare," said Sammy.

They looked down at Hare's body.

"No," said Sarah confidently. "The devil couldn't be in her shape. Look at her. She's much too beautiful for that."

They looked and all agreed without saying a word that whatever the role Hare would play in the story, it would not be one of evil.

"Mr. Bray said hares play tricks," said Kirsty. "Then perhaps the hare could play a trick on the witch. Or on her cat."

"Ooh, yes," said Jane. "Witches are really wicked. Perhaps the hare could be magic and turn her into a toad."

"Or perhaps," said Arthur, "the witch isn't wicked at all but she's going to be hanged because everybody thinks she is and the hare plays a trick on all the people so the witch gets away."

There was silence in the group for a minute. The sound of infant voices in the next room and a lawn mower on the school field could be heard clearly. Harry's group in the far corner of the room seemed also for a moment to be quiet. Then Freddy, for the first time, spoke.

"I don't think she ought to be magic. She should only do what hares do, otherwise it's a story about something else, not a hare."

"Where do we start, then?" said Harry to his group.

"Do we start with the nuclear holocaust?" said Raymond.

"Of course not," said Tim. "That's happened years before."

"We could describe how the hares became civilized," said Liz.

"Of course we couldn't," said Tim. "That would take months to do. We've only got today."

"We could describe the planet the extraterrestrials come from," said Derek. "And all about their spaceships and what the extraterrestrials looked like."

"Don't be daft," said Tim. "The story's supposed to be about the hares."

Harry managed to get a word in.

"Who's in charge of this group?" he said. "Me or you?"

"Only trying to help," said Tim.

Tracy spoke.

"I think this is silly. You're turning it into a stupid boys' story."

"Well, you needn't think we're going to have Mrs. Hare and all the little hares and Mr. Hare reading his newspaper," said Harry. "Why did you bother to join this group if you don't like what we're doing?"

"I joined to stop you writing a load of rubbish," said Tracy hotly. "I'm surprised you haven't got the hares playing football."

"That's a great idea," exclaimed Derek excitedly. "It could be the animal superbowl. Hare Wanderers versus Rabbit Rovers. And she could score the winning touchdown. A zigzag return from deep inside her own territory followed by a short TD pass from the six-yard line."

Tracy shot him a look of withering scorn and they all fell silent at the same time as the other group. Infant voices and the mower sounded very clear. Then Jenny, quiet till now, dropped her suggestion into the pool.

"I don't think we ought to have all this spaceship and other planets stuff in," she said. "Or football. And we shouldn't turn them into humans either. I don't think any of that's got anything to do with hares. But I do think it's got to be a story where the hare is a leader, like she is in what Harry and Tim said. But does she lead the hares against all the other animals or does she lead all the other animals against the humans?"

"How are you getting on?" said Sarah to Harry at break.

"Not bad," said Harry. "We've had a lot of arguments. But we've more or less sorted ourselves out now. We've decided the hare is going to lead all the other animals against the humans because they're trying to drive them out from where they live so they can build something. I don't know what yet, but Derek wants it to be a spaceport. What about you?"

"I suppose it's all right," said Sarah. "We've given up the idea of the witch's familiar. The hare's going to trick all the people who want to kill this old lady who they think is a witch. But she's just a friend of all the animals and not a witch at all. Though she can do magic. And she tells the future, like Old Mother Shipton Granny used to

talk about. Anyway, Hare fools the humans so the old lady's saved."

"I like it," said Harry. "Can we use that bit about the one human being friendly to the animals?"

"And can we have the bit about the humans driving the animals away?" said Sarah.

"We'll end up with two stories the same," said Harry.

"Why not?" said Sarah. "Better still, why don't we all join together again?"

"That's right," said Harry. "We'll all work on just the one story."

So they told Mr. Bray that when break was over the two groups would join together again. And no, they didn't want any help; they could all work on their own and they'd come up with a full story by the end of the day.

Mr. Bray breathed a sigh of relief. Mrs. Hoskins could go back to the younger children and he could have a rare chance to do his paperwork. God knows he sorely needed it.

Harry and Sarah explained the common ground between the two groups. Everybody seemed happy. Suddenly, with all fifteen in agreement, the story flowed. Everybody put in suggestions; fifteen voices raised themselves in excited discussion. When they knew the outline of the story, they divided it up into fifteen parts; each pupil now had one part to prepare. And until a quarter to three to do it. Then Mr. Bray, Mrs. Hoskins, and all the infants would meet in the tiny hall with its high, tie-beamed ceiling to listen as each part was read out in turn. Afterward, they would all go outside and watch while Harry buried the hare.

Mr. Bray was very happy about this.

"We'll have each part written out neatly and decorated and displayed on the wall," he said. Even as he spoke, he wondered whether he should not have suggested they put the story on the word processor. Then he had another idea. "I'll get the whole story really nicely typed and then I'll take it to the Teachers' Center in town and have it made up into a proper book. All your names will be on it. And we'll give a copy each to your parents and have some on sale in the Teachers' Center so a lot of people will read it. You'll be quite famous."

"So will the hare," said Sarah.

For the rest of the day the children wrote. Some sat at the tables in the classroom; some sprawled out on their tummies in the quiet corner. Others went out in the sunshine and sat under the horse-chestnut tree in the field; yet others leaned up against the jungle gym in the playground. Those who finished first helped those who were slower. Some wrote out every word they were going to say; others worked it all out in their heads and just wrote down a few words to remind themselves. The air in and around the school crackled with concentration.

And all the time Hare lay on the cloth spread over the table, and sometimes children—as if to remind themselves—came up to her, touched her, looked at her beauty, and thought about her onetime strength.

Quarter to three. Thankfully Mr. Bray finished writing out the answer to the latest letter from County Hall. Mrs. Hoskins shepherded the infants into the hall and the junior class stood facing them, each one clutching a piece of paper. Harry brought Hare in, still wrapped in the cloth, and reverently placed her on the table in front of them. Sarah spoke to the infants.

"This is a story we've made up about this hare. Not just any hare but this one. We're going to read it to you now and I'm going to start."

She cleared her throat and began to read from her paper in a high, ringing voice.

Still the animals huddled together in the blackness. Hare lifted her head and looked around. The sight was more than she could take in. She shook her head in puzzlement. Something was different. Something inside her mind was changing, growing stronger with every second. She now knew that there were other animals besides herself. This had never been so before. In life she had only known that there were some things to fear and other things not to. That was all the knowledge she needed. But now she could rise up on her hind legs, look over the huge throng, and be sure that these creatures were all separate, all different.

Were all of them feeling this change? Was this what it meant to be dead? And Hare wondered. What was "being dead"? Was it the cause of the nameless fear that had kept her fighting all her life until her last encounter? Were all the animals with her now wondering the same thing? If they did, why were they not looking around like her, with wild surmise and the dawn of understanding in their eyes?

Why should her mind be full of thoughts like this (what were "thoughts"?) when the minds of all the other creatures obviously weren't?

No, there was a tremendous change taking place for Hare and she did not like it. She was deeply frightened.

Now Hare had a new thought that stirred her troubles further. Was it to be like this forever or were they later to arrive at some place in the light where her questions (what were "questions"?) might be answered?

THREE

Story

"This is the story of the great Queen of the Hares, so great that she was just called 'Hare.' If any animal said 'Hare,' everybody would know who that animal meant. And also it is the story of Dame Isabel, the Wisewoman who lived in a cottage in a clearing in the woods at the top of the valley. She could talk to the animals, do magic spells, and see the future. Of all the animals that lived, Hare was Dame Isabel's favorite and of all humans Dame Isabel was the only one Hare knew or trusted."

Sarah paused here and looked round the room—at Harry sitting at the far end of the line of storytellers (he was due to finish it) and the thirteen others all with their sheets of paper and at the infants still wondering what to expect. Mr. Bray and Mrs. Hoskins looked back at Sarah encouragingly. But Sarah hadn't dried up. Part of her was still slightly sore about starting the story. It had been her idea in the first place, but the way the story had turned out she didn't, in the end, get any of the action. Still, she was trying to make the most of what she had got.

"One day," she at last continued, "Dame Isabel called Hare to her. 'Hare,' she said, 'last night I had a dream. I dreamed that men came to the valley where we live and started to cut down the trees and rip up the grass and drive all the living things away. Every living thing that did not escape, they killed. Every plant that was not ripped up, they burned. Then they came to my cottage and they set fire to it. They dragged me out and were going to kill me because they said I was a friend to the animals and was in their way. Then they slung a noose over the branch of a tree and lifted me up. They were about to hang me. And as they put the noose around my neck, I saw before me a terrible vision of the future. I saw huge towers and domes and great slab-sided skyscrapers where the fields and trees used to be. Everything we know and love was gone forever. Then I woke up.'

" 'But, Dame Isabel,' said Hare, 'that was only a dream.'

" 'When I dream so clearly,' said Dame Isabel, 'it is a warning of what might come to pass. Something dreadful is about to happen. We must all be on our guard.'

"Then Hare went away and told all the other animals what Dame Isabel had said. Some laughed because they thought it was just a silly dream, but others were very worried. They had all lived together in the valley for years and years, generations of animals happily getting along together. Surely it was not all about to come to an end?"

Sarah sat down, wishing she could go on for longer. Derek stood up.

After his wishes first of all for some science fiction and then for some football had been thwarted, Derek had felt sulky about the whole thing. The story seemed to be taking shape in a way he didn't like and there didn't seem much he could do about it. Then he saw a way of writing about some of the things he wanted to, so he claimed the second spot after Sarah.

"There was this big city a few miles away and it was the capital of the country. The President of this country, he got all his generals and scientists and builders around him and he said, 'We are the top country in the world and there's no one left to fight. So now we're going to conquer space. How long will it take to build a fleet of

spaceships, fully armed with rockets and lasers and carrying twenty thousand soldiers that can go to Mars and be sure of capturing it?'

"The chief scientist got his calculator and did some calculations. Then he said, 'We can build a fleet of spaceships in a year, but we need to build a proper spaceport as well. The spaceships will be powered by atomic reactors, so there will be a lot of radioactivity. That means the spaceport we build has to be a long way from the city. But we haven't got anywhere to build it that I can think of.'

" 'Oh, yes, we have,' said the Prime Minister, who had been listening all this time very carefully. 'There's that wooded valley a few miles from the city where nobody lives except a few animals and that daft old bat Dame Isabel. Nobody cares about her. She's off her rocker, thinking she can talk to animals. We can soon get rid of that crowd.'

" 'That's settled, then,' said the President. 'I'll expect you to get on with building the spaceport and the spaceships and be ready to take off for Mars this time next year.'

" 'That doesn't give us much time,' said the chief of the builders.

" 'We'll start clearing the place straight away,' said the top general. 'You can get all your steam shovels and backhoes and things ready now.' "

Derek sat down. Relief shone from his face. He'd got his space travel bit in and was well pleased.

Sammy, the smallest girl there, stood up. She had needed some help with her piece. Sarah had been very good to her.

"One day Hare saw some men in the wood and they were chopping trees down and then they killed some squirrels and some birds. So Hare said, 'Dame Isabel was right and we are going to be driven away. I must call a meeting of all the animals, which I can do anytime I like because I am the Queen.'

"So she called all the animals and birds to a clearing in the trees and they all sat around in a big circle while Hare told them what she had seen.

" 'There's nothing to worry about,' said the rabbits. 'We can just dig deep burrows in the ground and they will never find us.'

" 'That's right,' said the badgers. 'So can we. When we are all hiding in our sets, no humans can come anywhere near us.'

" 'We can fly very high,' said the birds. 'Once we're up there, we can stay up there and the humans can never reach us.'

" 'Well, we've nothing to be afraid of,' said the otters. 'All we have to do is to stay underwater. Then we will be safe.'

"When she heard all this, Hare was very angry. 'Don't be silly,' she said. 'We can't all dig like rabbits and badgers and can't all fly like birds or swim and stay underwater like otters. And anyway, wherever we go the humans will find us because they have clever nasty ways which we do not understand.'

"Then all the animals were very sad and said to Hare, 'What do we do then?' So Hare said, 'Leave me alone and I will think of a plan.' "

Sammy sat down, looking very pleased with herself, and smiled at Sarah. Sarah smiled back.

Now Freddy stood up. He had been very sure that the story should not have things in it that real hares couldn't do. But already the story had grown in such a way as to make that impossible. Even so, he was determined to be as accurate as he could.

"Hare wanted to be alone because that's what hares are like," he said. "They think best when they are on their own, especially if they can have a good run around first. Anyway, Hare, she ran around the fields and up and down the hills and all through the woods. She ran around in circles and she zigzagged all over the place. But she didn't get any good ideas at all. So she said to herself, 'I must go and see Dame Isabel. Perhaps she can help me. I know she can see the future. If she can tell me exactly what is going to happen, perhaps I can find a way to stop it.'

"But when she got to Dame Isabel's house she saw that it was burning and Dame Isabel was hanging from the branch of the biggest tree in the wood. So Hare jumped up the trunk of the tree and stepped out onto the branch and saw that Dame Isabel wasn't dead yet. So she leaned over and bit through the rope with her long teeth. Not all the way through but just enough so the rope would break slowly. Then Hare jumped back to the ground and stood below Dame Isabel to catch her when the rope broke.

"When the rope snapped and Hare had caught her, Dame Isabel opened her eyes and said, 'Thank you, Hare. You were only just in time. Hundreds of soldiers rushed into the clearing, set fire to my little cottage, dragged me out, and strung me up, just as they did in my dream. Why are they doing this to us? What have we done to deserve it? There's nothing we can do at all. Now you see my dream has come true.'

" 'No, it hasn't,' said Hare. 'They thought they had killed you. But they didn't. I stopped it. And if I stopped them once, I can stop them again.'

" 'Do you really think so, Hare?' said Dame Isabel.

" 'I know so,' said Hare."

Freddy's turn was finished. He was satisfied with the

way he had pictured Hare. She may have done a lot of unharelike things, but she had done them in a harelike way.

Jenny rose to her feet—a quiet and serious girl with long, straight black hair. Like Freddy she had been very sure about what sorts of things should go in the story. She wanted Hare to show herself as a leader and this part of the story let Hare be just that.

"Hare laid Dame Isabel down on the ground under the tree and made her as comfortable as possible with pillows of bracken. From where they were they could see the cottage still burning. Dame Isabel was very ill and Hare knew something would have to be done or she would die. So Hare ran at her top speed through the woods and fields calling all the animals and birds. Soon they had gathered all the herbs they could find that would make Dame Isabel well again and brought them to her. Dame Isabel knew all about herbs and had taught the animals, so now they were repaying her.

" 'Thank you,' said Dame Isabel when she had recovered. 'You have let me live. But until the men go away and we can stay here in peace forever, I shall not get up from my bed here on the ground.'

" 'But, Dame Isabel,' cried all the animals, 'without you and Hare together we have no hope.'

"Then Hare spoke. 'I have thought of a plan,' she said.

"Now the animals were all very quiet as they listened to Hare.

" 'What we need are tricks and magic. Because I am a hare, I can play tricks. We hares are known for it. But I cannot do magic. Some humans think we can, but they are wrong. Dame Isabel can still do magic, though, even if she can't get up yet. So what I think is this.'

" 'Nothing too hard, please, Hare,' said Dame Isabel.

" 'For you, this is easy,' said Hare. 'You must change my shape so I look like you. Humans believe hares are shape-changers, but they are not. But they can be changed by people who have magic.'

" 'And what good will that do?' said Dame Isabel. 'Why turn a great strong animal like you into a frail old lady like me?'

" 'You will only change my shape,' said Hare. 'So I can still run like a hare and think like a hare. Then I will go into the city and find out what the humans are doing.'

" 'They will kill you,' said all the animals.

" 'No, they won't,' said Hare. 'First, they will be scared stiff when they see me because they think Dame Isabel is dead. Then, when they try to, they won't catch me because I will play tricks on them and get away. And when I come back I will have found out how we can beat off the humans.'

"The animals and birds were very pleased with this plan and they cheered Hare very loudly. But Dame Isabel looked tired and said, 'Well, I suppose I've got to summon up all my strength and make a spell.' However, there was a twinkle in her eye.

"She lifted both her hands, said some strange words no one understood, then cried, 'Oh, great Queen of the Hares, take on the shape of your old friend Dame Isabel. But do not take on her frailty. Keep all your hare's strength and your hare's cunning.'

"There was a sudden flash of bright light and all the animals and birds gasped. For where Hare had stood a second before, now stood another Dame Isabel, wearing the same old black cloak and with the same old gray hair.

" 'No time to lose,' said the new Dame Isabel, and she was away. But she didn't hobble like an old woman. She ran off in a straight line as fast as a hare."

Jenny sat down looking a little embarrassed, because

halfway through she had realized that her section was twice as long as anyone else's so far. She needn't have worried.

Arthur, a pale-faced boy, pudgy for his age, rose to take Jenny's place. He had wanted Hare to play tricks and had made sure that his section of the story contained some.

"Hare raced for miles and miles across the country. She didn't like having the black cloak on, but Dame Isabel had magicked it so that it was very light. So it wasn't too bad. After hours of running she saw on the horizon something she had never seen before. Great towers and huge buildings. Skyscrapers with helicopters flying around them. Long bridges carrying motorways and railways. It was the first time she had seen a human city. But she didn't let it frighten her and just kept on running until she reached its borders.

"When she was inside the city, she looked in wonder at all the shops and the people and the rapid transit jet buses they all traveled in. But she didn't stop for long, because she wanted to find the Government Building where the President and all the generals were.

"In the very middle of the city she found the Government Building. It towered over her, big and gray and very forbidding-looking. All around it stood soldiers guarding it with submachine guns. At first Hare felt a bit scared when she saw them. Then she remembered why she was there, marched up to the most frightening-looking soldier of the lot—who happened to be guarding the main entrance—and said, 'I want to see the President.'

" 'Go away, you old fool,' said the soldier. 'No one sees the President without an appointment.'

" 'He'll see me,' said Hare, 'because I am the one that he had killed come back to haunt him.'

"Hare looked the soldier straight in the eyes. He screamed

with fear and fainted with shock. He had been one of those who had burned the cottage down and tried to hang Dame Isabel. Hare walked straight past him while he was still out cold on the ground and into the building. She walked cautiously down miles of corridors that never seemed to lead anywhere and was beginning to give up hope when she came to a big door that said on it PRESIDENT. KEEP OUT. CONFERENCE IN PROGRESS. So she opened it.

"The President sat at the head of a big table. Down each side sat all his generals, scientists, and builders. Nobody saw Hare enter. They went on talking.

" 'How are the spaceships coming on?' he said to the chief scientist.

" 'We have one finished already, sir,' said the chief scientist. 'Three are nearly done and we've made a start on six more. But we still haven't got anywhere to test them.'

" 'How are you getting on with building the spaceport?' the President asked the chief builder.

" 'We haven't started yet, sir,' said the chief builder. 'The army still hasn't cleared the land for us to get on with it.'

"The President looked very angry and turned to the top general.

" 'Why not?' he demanded.

" 'We're doing our best, sir,' said the general. 'These things take time.'

" 'Not good enough,' roared the President. 'Just get a move on, will you?'

" 'But we've already got rid of some of the animals,' said the top general. 'And we've burned down the old lady's cottage and executed her as an enemy of the state.'

" 'That's better,' said the President. 'But remember. I want some action and I want some results.'

"Then he saw Hare.

" 'Who's that?' he shouted.

"The generals looked up and saw Hare. They all screamed with terror and clung trembling to each other.

" 'It's the old woman we hanged,' stuttered one.

" 'It's a ghost come back to haunt us,' stammered another.

" 'Don't be silly,' said the chief scientist. 'There's no such things as ghosts. It's just an old-age pensioner come in for a bit of heat.'

" 'Seize her,' commanded the President.

"Everyone now ran after Hare, thinking they could easily catch her. But Hare led them a dance down corridors, up staircases, nipping out of corners where they didn't expect her, doubling back, and leading them around and around till all the men were exhausted and she was laughing fit to burst.

"Then she ran full tilt out of the Government Building, straight past the soldiers, who were all too surprised to stop her, through the streets of the city, out again into the country, and didn't stop until she reached the place where Dame Isabel still lay under the tree."

Arthur's contribution had been as long as Jenny's, but he didn't look at all embarrassed. He'd enjoyed it and wished he'd spun it out a bit longer—especially the chase through the city and back to the valley. However, some of the children were getting restless and Mr. Bray was shooting "Hurry-it-up" glances at Harry and Sarah. Harry and Sarah saw them and shrugged their shoulders. The story wasn't halfway through yet.

Liz—tall, skinny, and fair-haired—stood up. Mr. Bray's glances weren't lost on her. She began reading very fast indeed. It seemed a long time now since her idea of describing how the hares had become civilized. But she still liked the idea and in her part of the story she had resolved to put down a few ideas of how it might have happened.

"Hare got all the animals together and told them what she had seen and heard," Liz said. "She told them that the humans would be there very soon to start building and so they would have to be ready to defend themselves.

" 'How can we do that?' they all cried. 'We are only tiny and there are millions of them.'

"But Hare told them to be quiet while she spoke.

" 'Do you remember how when we first heard about Dame Isabel's dream you said you would all be all right because the rabbits and badgers would dig burrows, the birds would fly high, and the otters would stay underwater?'

" 'We do, Hare,' they all groaned. 'And we are very sorry because we know now how silly that was.'

" 'What you *said* was silly. But what you *do* isn't. We can use all those things against the humans—enough to stop them from overrunning our home. First, the rabbits and the badgers will creep out at night onto the open land between here and the city. Then they will start digging all the burrows that they can. Not to live in—as soon as you have finished one, you leave it and start another.'

" 'We will, Hare,' said the rabbits.

" 'But why?' said the badgers.

" 'Simple,' said Hare. 'When you have finished, there will be this crisscross of little tunnels just underneath the surface of the ground. So when the humans bring all their big machines to start building, the ground will be weak and they will all fall in. It will take them days to get them out again.'

" 'That's brilliant, Hare,' said the rabbits.

" 'Let's get started,' said the badgers.

"Hare went on. 'The birds will be ready the minute I tell them to take off and fly as high as they can.'

" 'We will, Hare,' said all the birds together. 'But why?'

" 'The big birds, like the hawks, will swoop on the men as they come near and do to them exactly what they do to all the animals they catch. The small birds will carry stones and pebbles in their beaks, wait until they are right over the humans, and then drop them. Try to aim for their heads and especially their eyes. And also, if you can, drop the stones in their machines so they will not work.'

" 'That's the best idea yet, Hare,' said the birds excitedly.

"Hare turned to the otters. 'You,' she said, 'must lurk underneath the water in the streams that flow along the valley.'

" 'We will, Hare,' said the otters. 'But why?'

" 'Because the humans' top general will send soldiers in to destroy us. The best way in to surprise us is along the streams. They will wade along them in single file. They want to surprise us—but we must surprise them. Your teeth can bite a fish in two with no trouble. So you can see what you can do to the legs of the soldiers. This is how we stop the humans coming onto our land.'

" 'Fantastic,' said the otters.

"When Hare had finished speaking, the animals cheered her louder than ever. And Dame Isabel said, 'Well done, Hare. By the way, I forgot to change you back again.'

"There was another bright flash of light and there stood the Queen of the Hares again, just as they had always known her."

Liz's section ended. She sat down and smoothed back her fair hair. She was pleased with herself. Her ideas had set up the next part of the story very neatly.

Emma stood up, demure and pretty. She had been cross with Sarah at the very beginning in the first group. Sarah had not liked Emma's objecting to her first idea and Emma had not liked being taken no notice of. Especially when Roy said the same thing and everybody listened. Since then, she had been thinking a lot. Still waters run deep. This placid girl had listened to Liz's ideas and turned them into action. Then, seeing that Roy was of the same mind, she had gone up to him and they had worked out their piece together.

"Straightaway the rabbits and badgers set about their work. Hundreds of rabbits burrowed into the ground and by next morning they had made an invisible spider's web of tunnels only just under the ground. Scores of badgers dug as well; their burrows were like underground pits in between the rabbit warrens. The passages stretched for miles. All night the birds waited in the branches of the trees for Hare's signal in case the humans came when it was still dark. The otters crouched by the riverbank, ready to slide into the water as soon as Hare gave the word. But all night long nothing happened.

"Next morning, as the sun rose, Hare looked out across the land toward the city.

" 'They will come this morning,' she said.

"She sent the skylarks, the highest-flying birds, to look out for the humans. They took off and soon were tiny dots in the blue sky. After a while they returned.

" 'Many humans with giant machines—bulldozers and cranes and tractors—are on their way. Thousands of soldiers are marching along beside them. They will be here soon.'

"Suddenly, from out of their holes in the ground, all the rabbits appeared, followed by the badgers. They were all filthy with dirt and could hardly stand for tiredness.

" 'They are coming, Hare,' they chorused. 'We felt the ground shake above us and we knew we would have to come out or be crushed as the machines fell through.'

" 'Be ready,' Hare called out to the birds and otters.

"Now they could see all the men and their machines coming along very fast—nearer and nearer. And then . . ."

Emma sat down suddenly.

Roy stood up. He and Emma had worked hard to get the changeover right in this part of the story.

"Suddenly all the tractors and backhoes started disappearing. They fell through the ground where the rabbits and badgers had weakened it and great clouds of dust hid them from view.

"Then Hare shouted 'GO' at the top of her voice and the birds took off. The kestrels, falcons, and buzzards flew up high and then swooped down, pecking at faces and eyes and scratching deep wounds with their talons. All the other birds dropped stones. The thrushes and starlings dropped pebbles, the sparrows and wrens tiny flints that were sharp and hurt where they hit. The bigger stones knocked some humans out and bruised others. And some stones got into the works of the diggers and fouled them all up.

"The men were furious. The top general shouted to his soldiers, 'No more of this nonsense. Get in there and finish them off. Wade along the stream and take them by surprise.'

"Then Hare shouted 'GO' to the otters and they slipped into the water and waited. The first soldiers came wading along in their jungle-green battle dress, holding their automatic rifles above their heads, and the otters, unseen, sprang at their legs. They bit deep into leg after leg with their sharp fangs. There were shouts of rage, pain, and terror from the soldiers as the water turned red with blood, because they had no idea what was happening.

"Soon they had all run away. The soldiers and the builders escaped back into the city. They left the steam shovels and bulldozers behind where they were stuck in the ground.

"The animals watched them go, hardly able to believe what they saw. When it was quite certain no human would return, the animals and birds let out great shrieks, screams,

howls, screeches, squawks, and hoots of joy. They climbed trees to make sure that the humans had really gone. They chattered and chirruped to each other in disbelief. Then they danced in sheer delight around and around in great circles until they fell down exhausted. But not for long. Within a few minutes they had all got up again and started the biggest party the valley had ever seen. They didn't go to sleep till dawn—but after that they were dead to the world for two days."

Roy's contribution was over. Together he and Emma had organized what they thought was the most exciting part of the story so far. "Beat that," he said to himself as he sat down.

Kirsty's turn. She cast a broad smile over the rows of children, who were now all looking as if the whole thing was a bit too much for them. This didn't deter her in the least.

"When the animals and birds woke up and remembered what had happened they were really happy. They rushed around the valley again, shouting, 'We won. We won. We're safe,' at the tops of their voices. But Hare and Dame Isabel knew better and talked quietly together.

" 'They will come back,' said Hare. 'They won't take this lying down. They won't like being made fools of by a bunch of animals.'

" 'You are right,' said Dame Isabel. 'I fear for the future.'

" 'When they come back,' said Hare, 'we will fight the last battle. How are we going to hold out for a second time?'

" 'I do not know, Hare,' said Dame Isabel. 'My poor old brain won't work anymore.'

" 'So far we have got by with your magic and my tricks,' said Hare. 'We need more than that to make our place safe forever. We need tricks and magic so strong that they may be the end of you and me.'

"Dame Isabel started to laugh. 'I see the future again,' she said. 'I see our animals living here in our valley, forever in perfect peace, with no humans to disturb them. I see them all happy, without a care in the world.' Then her voice became sad. 'But I do not see you and me with them.'

"Hare said, 'The humans will not be content until they have built their spaceport. As far as I am concerned they can build what they like. But why do they have to build it here?'

"She thought for a long time. Then she said, 'Dame Isabel, I am going on a journey. You may not hear from me for a long while. We have some time to prepare for the last battle. It will take the humans days to pull their steam shovels out of the ground. So when I am needed, I will be back.'

" 'I understand,' said Dame Isabel. 'We will wait for you to return. I shall tell the others not to worry.'

"That night Hare left the valley where she had lived for so many years and traveled over strange roads and fields, past the homes of countless animals and humans who were not friendly to her. She had many adventures and many narrow escapes, but she kept on going because she knew what it was she had to find.

"One day she was toiling up a long, grassy slope. Far away she could hear a dull roaring noise. Though she did not know it, it was the sea. At the top of the slope, along the horizon, she saw rolls and rolls of barbed wire. It stretched for miles, as if someone with a sharp pencil had scribbled on the blue sky. She reached the top of the slope, picked her way carefully through the barbed wire, and looked over. She was at the edge of a cliff. Below was a land such as she had never seen before. Nobody and nothing lived there. Gray, dead rocks and barren soil stretched away on either side as far as she could see. There were huge black holes in the ground from which billowed stinking smoke and steam. Ruined buildings with broken chimneys were dotted higgledy piggledy around. It was an awful place. Beyond it stretched the gray, sullen sea.

"A seagull flew down and stood beside her. 'Terrible, isn't it,' he said. 'Humans used to live here. They had homes here and factories and mines where they took stuff out of the ground and made things with it. Then they seemed to get tired of it all and left. Since then it has just fallen to pieces. Nobody lives here because the land is poisoned. I come here as little as I can. I only stopped because I am passing through and was so surprised to see anyone here.'

"Hare said, 'This is what I have been looking for. Thank you, seagull.'

"She turned around and bounded away from that dreadful wasteland and didn't stop running until she was back in the valley and standing next to Dame Isabel."

Kirsty sat down, her face smiling more broadly than ever. The last part of the story needed to be set up properly and she felt quite sure that she had done it as well as anyone could.

Raymond now rose to his feet, clutching his piece of paper nervously. He was the youngest and smallest boy and had a slight stammer as well. The color had drained from his face and his hair was the color of old straw. He had forced himself to ask the first question in Harry's group that morning and still hadn't quite got over being slapped down by Tim—even though Tim had come over to help him in the afternoon.

"All the animals were very frightened," he said. "The

men had pulled all the steam shovels and bulldozers out of the rabbit holes and were nearly ready to attack again. The animals were so pleased when they saw Hare approaching that they swarmed out of the wood to meet her and escort her the last few yards. Then they sat down in the clearing with Dame Isabel to hear what Hare had to say.

"Hare said, 'We all know what the humans want to build here, don't we?'

" 'Yes,' they all shouted. 'A silly spaceport. Why can't they be satisfied with what they've already got?'

" 'That's the difference between the humans and us,' said Hare. 'We want everything to stay as it is so we can live like we always do, but humans are always trying to do something new. They always want things to change. They try to find things out that we don't care about. They go to places that we wouldn't want to see at all. They're never content. Poor things, they can't help it. And we'll never change them.'

"The animals were sad to hear Hare say this.

" 'Is that all you've come back for?' shouted a big badger. 'Just to tell us it's no use fighting?'

" 'I didn't say that,' said Hare. 'What I said was that you can't stop humans being the way they are. We can't stop them building their spaceport. We just have to make sure they don't build it here. They can do all the things they want to as long as they don't upset others at the same time.'

" 'And where are they going to build their spaceport if it's not here?' said the badger.

" 'I've found the very place for them,' said Hare. 'A place they've ruined once already. A place where nothing and nobody lives so nobody's going to care. They can tidy up their own mess. They can build anything they like there, to their hearts' content.'

" 'I see,' said the badger. 'And you're just going up to all those generals and saying, "Please go away and build

where we tell you to." And they're going to say, "Of course, Hare. Sorry, Hare. Anything you say, Hare." '

" 'No,' said Hare. 'We have to *make* them build there.'

"Suddenly, all the animals stared in amazement. Dame Isabel was rising to her feet for the first time since Hare had rescued her. She stood up straight and tall and surveyed the animals with her clear gray eyes.

" 'There is one way we can do this,' she said. 'But it will be with the last magic I ever do and with perhaps the last tricks Hare will ever play.' "

Raymond's piece was over. Color came back to his cheeks and he sat down with beads of sweat on his forehead. Tim clapped his hands silently. Harry leaned over and patted Raymond on the shoulder.

Jane, whose opinions on witches had been changed considerably during the day, stood up to take Raymond's place.

"Dame Isabel looked very weak and frail and she held on to Hare for support.

" 'We have to do two things,' she said. 'First, we have to stop the men breaking in here again. Second, we have to lead them to the place Hare found.'

" 'That's right,' all the animals said.

" 'I can do magic for the first,' said Dame Isabel. 'I can use all the powers I have left to put an invisible wall, a tough transparent shield, all around our home that no one could get through. But it will only last for a short time. While we are secure, Hare has to lure the humans away so they follow her to the new place.'

" 'Can she do that?' said the badger.

" 'Hares have always been hunted,' said Dame Isabel. 'And they have always led their hunters a merry dance. This will be Hare's longest and most dangerous hunt of all. The humans will follow her to the end.'

"When the animals heard this they were very quiet and sad. They were upset by the thought that they might never see Hare and Dame Isabel again. But they knew that nothing else could save them.

" 'Dame Isabel is right,' said Hare. 'I am ready. And I am the Queen, so it is my duty.'

" 'Now let us all rest,' said Dame Isabel. 'Tomorrow will be the day when everything will be decided. Sleep well, all of you, and wake up refreshed in the morning.'

"All the animals and birds then went to their burrows, their nests, and their lairs and happily fell asleep. But Dame Isabel and Hare stayed awake all night, sitting side by side, saying nothing, but each thinking of what the next day might bring."

Jane sat down. The room was now very quiet.

It was Tim's turn. He stood up, his big dark eyes glaring fiercely. Things had changed a lot since he had laughed at Harry's first idea, not always to his liking. But there was going to be some action now, and he—and this he was sure of—was the best one to give it.

"The sun rose next morning and it was going to be a hot day. Long before the other animals woke up, Hare and Dame Isabel looked out toward where the humans were. They could see rows upon rows of steam shovels and bulldozers, not only those that had been pulled out of the ground but lots of new ones as well. They could see lines of soldiers ready for combat and helicopters ready to fly them in. Behind them, on top of a hill, were big guns ready to bombard them and tanks ready to flatten them. It was a terrible sight.

" 'How can my magic stand up against all that?' groaned Dame Isabel.

" 'Nothing in the world can stand up against your magic,' said Hare.

"Suddenly there was a great roar as all the diesel engines were started up at once.

" 'This is it,' shouted Hare.

"Everything began to come nearer—backhoes, soldiers, tanks. The noise was deafening. All the animals woke up and there was panic all around.

" 'NOW!' cried Hare.

"Dame Isabel stood up, threw her arms out wide, cried strange words Hare had never heard before and then—'I ask you, spirit that rules all animals and plants, to protect us now. Throw an invisible wall around our friends and our home so that the invader may not enter.'

"There was a tremendous flash of lightning, which hurled both Hare and Dame Isabel to the ground. The last rumble of thunder was dying away when they were able to struggle to their feet. They looked back and saw that the trees and fields behind them were still there but faint and misty. Their friends—badgers, rabbits, foxes, owls, woodpeckers—stood still in rows, staring at them like children looking through a window.

" 'This will not last long,' said Dame Isabel.

"The army in front of them still came nearer, as if nothing had happened.

" 'Now it is my turn,' cried Hare. 'I am the Queen of the Hares, so change me, Dame Isabel, so that everyone can see.'

"Dame Isabel stretched out her arms again and shouted yet more words Hare did not understand—then: 'BE the Queen of the Hares, as all your friends know you are.'

"Then Hare stood tall in front of the army. Between her ears was a crown of gold with green emeralds; her flowing robe, too, was gold but edged with the colors of the rainbow. She carried a scepter, which flashed fire and for a moment blinded the humans, who were still coming nearer.

"Now Hare's voice sounded over the noise of the approaching hosts.

" 'I am the Queen of all those you wish to destroy. But to kill them, you have to kill me first. Before you kill me, you must catch me. If you can do that, then we are not fit to stay in our valley and it is yours. If you cannot catch me, then you must think again.'

"The leading bulldozer driver said, 'What a load of rubbish,' and drove straight past Hare. Almost at once he hit the invisible wall at full speed. The digger was smashed to bits and caught fire. The driver was killed at once.

" 'You see?' said Hare.

"Suddenly, her royal robes were gone and she was just a hare again. Like a flash she was away.

"A great shout of anger sounded from all over the human hordes.

" 'After her,' came the cry as they lumbered into action. 'Chase her to the death.' "

Tim sat down and wiped his forehead with a tissue. The room was very hot and Mrs. Hoskins used the gap before Tracy stood up to open the windows wider. A cool breeze entered and with it the sounds of the outside world.

Tracy, like Tim, had a mind of her own and was not afraid to use it. She had red hair, blue eyes, and freckles. After she had been so forthright about what the story should *not* be, she had insisted on having for herself the climax of what it *ought* to be. And Harry and Sarah would have been very brave not to let her have her way.

"Hare ran as fast as her legs would carry her. First of all she dashed off in a straight line, to get herself as far away from the valley in as short a time as possible. Everything chased her—steam shovels, soldiers, tanks. The noise was tremendous. But however fast they went and no matter how much racket they made, Hare kept ahead of them.

"Now and again she looked back to see how her hunters

were getting on. Sometimes she let them come near her and they let out cries of triumph because they thought she was caught. But suddenly she would change direction and be off the other way before the humans could turn. Sometimes she hid and let the whole lot go right past her; then she would bob up behind them and laugh while they clumsily turned around and set off the other way.

"The humans began to get very cross. They started to argue among themselves. The bulldozer drivers shouted to the soldiers, 'You guys aren't worth much if you can't catch a little hare.' And the soldiers shouted back, 'We're on foot. You've got great diesel engines and still you can't come near her.'

"Then someone shouted, 'She's disappeared. We've lost her.' And then Hare would stand up on her hind legs in a completely different place from where they were looking, waggle her whiskers at them, and shout, 'Fooled you. You can't catch me.' Then she was off once more over the horizon and the chase started again.

"All the time she was getting nearer the sea and the dreadful poisoned place she had found on her earlier journey. The day drew on; the sun rose to its highest point and began to sink. Many, many miles had been covered. Hare began to tire and the beats from her great heart sounded loud in her ears. She was hot and weary. But still the hunters followed. However much she fooled them and led them a dance, they still kept on coming.

"Then, on the horizon, she saw the rolls of barbed wire. This was the place. Dead beat now, she struggled to the top of the rise and along the road that led past the place where she had met the seagull. She reached the barbed wire. Now she could hardly walk. She stumbled and fell against it and the barbs made long scratches along her body. The pain brought her to her senses again. She stood up on her hind legs, faced her pursuers, and said to herself, 'Now, Dame Isabel, just one last little piece of magic.' Somehow, all those miles away in the valley, Dame Isabel heard. 'BE the Queen of the Hares,' she cried for a second time, and willed the magic to happen with all her strength. And work it did. Once again Hare carried a scepter and wore a crown and a shining robe. The hunters stopped and blinked. The diesel engines were switched off.

" 'Look beyond the wire. Look at the mess you've left under the cliff,' cried Hare. 'That's the place where you should build your spaceport. Leave us to our lives. Build it here where you harm no one. Build it here on land you've already ruined. But leave my friends in peace, I beg of you.'

"Those were Hare's last words. Even her great heart could not keep going any longer. At the very last it gave out; her crown and robes disappeared; she fell dead, just a hare again, stretched out by the side of the road."

When Tracy finished, there was a complete and profound silence in the room. Every eye turned to the brown body lying on the cloth. Tracy sat down and furtively wiped her eyes. She had found the last few lines very difficult to get through. She prided herself on being a tough one and this had surprised her.

Harry stood up. The last words were to be his. Now that they were here, he felt slightly cheated. All the big action seemed to have gone by without him. That didn't seem right. After all, it had been his idea in the first place, his and Sarah's. He looked quickly down his sheet of paper and thought: *This doesn't add up to much.*

"All the hunters stood at the top of the rise. The builders cleared away the barbed wire. The soldiers ran past, set up their gear, and then abseiled down the cliff. The

builders and scientists picked their way down very slowly. At last they were all standing together in the wasteland by the sea.

" 'Well, there's one thing good about it,' said the builders. 'The ruins of the old buildings will make good filler for our concrete. That's always a problem.'

" 'We could keep supply routes open by sea,' said the soldiers. 'A place by the sea is easier to defend than one that's entirely inland.'

" 'It's always best to launch rockets over sea than over land,' said the scientists. 'We must think of the safety factor.'

" 'Well,' said the top general, 'this is where the spaceport is to be, then. All agreed?'

"Everybody did.

" 'What idiot suggested that other place anyway?' said the chief of the builders.

" 'It was the Prime Minister,' said the top general.

" 'That was the second Prime Minister before this one,' said the chief scientist. 'We got rid of him weeks ago. So we needn't worry on that score.'

" 'What shall we tell the President?' said the chief of the builders.

" 'You just leave the President to me,' said the top general. 'Who do you think runs this country, anyway?'

"So they all started work and completely forgot Hare lying dead by the side of the road.

"Many miles away Dame Isabel spoke to all the other animals and birds.

" 'We are safe now,' she said. 'Hare has done her work. But we shall never see her again.'

"All the animals and birds were very distressed. In hearing that Hare was dead, they quite forgot to be happy at being left in peace.

" 'What shall we do, Dame Isabel?' they cried. 'We

should bring her back and bury her here, where she lived all her life.'

" 'We cannot do that,' said Dame Isabel. 'But we can send our longest-flying birds out to her with flowers to remember her by.'

"So two swallows, who would soon be flying to Africa for the winter, took off. One had buttercups in his beak; the other cow parsley in hers. They flew all the way to where Hare was, laid the flowers by her side, and then continued their journey.

" 'Still,' said a badger when the swallows had left, 'we still have you, Dame Isabel.'

" 'Not for long,' said Dame Isabel. 'I have used up all my powers. Soon I shall follow Hare. You will have to sort things out on your own in future.'

" 'We will,' said the animals. 'We owe it to you and Hare.'

"Then they stood in silence to remember the leader who had saved them. They vowed that their land would stay free of humans forever.

"Meanwhile, back at the new site for the spaceport, work went on. But after the swallows had left, the body of Hare still lay unnoticed by the side of the road. Then a boy and a girl passed by on their way to school. They saw the body and stopped. At first they thought it was a cat. Then they thought it was a rabbit. Then they saw it was a hare. They saw its brown back and white front, the lovely golden-brown on its back legs and its great long ears. They saw the scratches on its side and wondered how they had got there. They picked up the buttercups and cow parsley and won-dered who had laid them there so carefully. Then they decided to pick the hare up and carry it to school so they could write a story about it. So that is what they did."

Harry sat down. The fifteen storytellers looked at each other with great satisfaction. Mr. Bray said, 'Well, I'm sure we've all enjoyed that lovely story about such a clever animal, haven't we." The infants still looked bemused. Mr. Bray felt somehow inadequate. What had happened deserved more and better words than that, but he just didn't have them.

Outside in the playground, groups of mothers, some with baby carriages and strollers, were gathering. Mr. Bray nodded to Mrs. Hoskins and she led the younger children out. Mr. Bray turned to the others.

"I meant what I said," he told them. "We'll get it properly typed and then have it printed and bound at the Teachers' Center. It will be something to treasure all your lives."

"Sir," said Harry, "what about the hare?"

"Of course, Harry," said Mr. Bray. "I hadn't forgotten."

They all went outside. Mr. Bray picked up a spade from the toolshed, and led them to a sunny spot in the corner of the school field. Sarah carried the body of the hare, still wrapped up in its cloth.

"Dig here," said Mr. Bray, and gave Harry the spade.

Harry dug into the cool, dark earth. The rest watched as a mound of glistening clods rose by the side of the hole he was making. Harry was an expert digger—he'd had good practice at home on the farm. Soon the hole was three feet deep and long enough for Hare to be laid in without touching the sides.

Sarah turned the cloth back for one last look at the whiskered face, the long ears, the glassy eyes. Then she laid Hare gently on the floor of the hole. Each child took it in turns to throw a piece of earth in the grave; Mr. Bray—and then Mrs. Hoskins, who joined them when all the younger children were safely on their way home—threw earth in as well. Then Harry carefully filled the hole, leaving a dark mound on the grass.

All seventeen stood around the grave silently. The odd sniff and nose-blow sounded. Then Sarah broke the silence.

"We'll make a gravestone out of wood," she said.

"Sounds a bit crazy," said Tim.

"No, it isn't," said Harry. "I can carve it with a chisel. I'll put 'RIP the Queen of the Hares.' Then we'll always remember."

"That's what we'll call the story," said Sarah. " 'The Queen of the Hares.' "

FOUR

Choice

Hare stood on her hind legs and looked around her yet again. Light was spreading. She could now pick out details of her surroundings and begin to make some sense of them.

It was time, she felt, to solve the question once and for all of whether the other creatures now felt the same as she did. A small yellow monkey with big eyes ringed with brown like huge saucers cavorted beside her.

"What is this?" she said to him. "Where are we going?"

The monkey turned sightless eyes toward her, chattered incomprehensibly, and bounded away.

She turned to a wolf but got no answer from him either. In despair she crossed to one of her own kind, a big brown buck hare with a broken ear.

"What's all this about?" she said.

He looked at her blankly with his bulging eyes, gave her a hard slap with his right paw, and leapt away. In a moment he was lost to sight in the great mass of animals.

Hare sat down to think. Why did they all seem so stupid? What was this terrifying change that had come over her? And what—this was the really momentous thing—had she been doing just now when she tried to get sense out of the other animals? She had been *talking*. Using *words*. Words, like thoughts, like questions, were not what animals had. She listened. There were brays, neighs, roars, barks, chirrups, squeaks. But no words. She had something none of the other animals had. Why? What had put the words there? Why did she need them? She didn't before.

Thoughts, questions, words. And then something else. Memories. She remembered the red beast. Running alongside it—and then into it. That was why she was here. She *remembered*. The last thing in her life.

But wait a minute. She saw the red beast like a picture in her mind. But there were other pictures in her mind—strong, vivid ones that made no sense but that showed things that seemed to have happened after the red beast.

This was impossible. Of being a leader to great numbers of animals, many of whom she knew ought to be her enemies. Of a friendship with a human being of great wisdom. Of standing tall and proud in a shining robe with a crown on her head. Of long journeys into danger and of a final hunt where she willingly gave her life up so that other animals might live. Of being Queen.

She looked again over the heaving crowd of creatures. New feelings came, which were the most surprising of all. She was sorry for them. She felt responsible. Most frightening of all—she felt somehow as if she was their leader.

The new light hurt Hare's eyes. When she was used to it, she looked back to see—deep into the deepest space that could be imagined, losing itself in the empty blue of sheer distance. She turned the other way, to where the animals were headed. The floor on which they moved was gold; as Hare looked farther, she realized they were all on a bright golden platform hanging alone in this huge expanse of space. Its horizon in front of her shaded into a deep purple, like an impossibly rich curtain. In this curtain there was a door that towered above the animals, of the same burnished gold as the floor. The animals moved, tranced, toward the door; as Hare watched, it began to swing open. The leaders went through. The others followed.

Am I to go with them? Hare stood on her hind legs watching, not knowing what she was supposed to do.

"Hare."

The voice seemed to come from all around her. She half heard, half felt it. Neither high nor deep, neither loud nor soft, it filled her whole being. With it came a feeling of great peace. She looked about her.

"Yes?" she said.

"Hare, come with me," the voice said.

"Where are you?" said Hare. "How can I come with you if I cannot see you?"

"You will see," said the voice.

Hare now felt something rest on her shoulder. Was it a hand? A giant paw? It guided her forward to a high place, like a balcony. Below them the seemingly endless stream of animals poured through the open golden door.

"Can you see me now?" said the voice.

"No," said Hare, "but I know you are there."

For there was a presence next to her: a presence of great strength, comfort, and wisdom.

"I am the overseer of this place," said the voice. "I have waited for you and sought you out. You are the Queen of the Hares."

Hare was angry at this.

"Don't mock me," she said. "I am a hare; nothing but an ordinary hare. And I don't know where I am."

"This is the place where the animals come for the afterlife," said the overseer. "If you like, it is the animals' heaven. Each day new creatures come from earth; each day the door opens and they pour through, adding still more to the unimaginable throngs inside."

Hare was still angry.

"Why aren't I with them, then?" she said.

"Because you are different," said the overseer. "You are the Queen."

"How can I be different? I'm only a hare. I've just seen another one. I tried to talk to him. He could have been my brother."

"He was not," said the overseer.

The last arrival had gone. Silently the door began to swing to.

"NO," roared the overseer. "DON'T CLOSE IT YET."

"Why not?" said Hare.

"Because you may use it," said the overseer.

"Why not now?"

"Because there is another place for animals," said the overseer. "You have to be shown it. But before that, I want you to see inside the first one."

The pressure on Hare's shoulder guided her to the open door.

"Don't cross the threshold," said the overseer, "or there is no coming back. Just look."

Hare looked. The view was limitless. Wide plains of ever-renewing grass for grazing. Numberless trees for nesting in and climbing. Rivers, seas, and lakes for swimming in. And all was thick with animals, birds, reptiles—grazing, flying aimlessly, sunning themselves. Millions upon millions of creatures of every sort as far as the eye could see and then beyond.

Hare looked, took it all in, and considered.

"That's where I should be," she said at length. "Why won't you let me go?"

"You have a choice," said the overseer. "Alone of all the animals who arrived today, you have a choice."

"I don't understand," said Hare.

"Come with me again," said the overseer.

They descended the steps from the balcony and Hare was led to the other side of the great platform, where there was another door, also made of burnished gold. But this door was much, much smaller. There was only room for one at a time to pass through. There were letters carved on it that Hare could not read.

"Go in there," said the overseer.

"But will I be able to come out again once I cross the threshold?" Hare asked.

"This is not like the first place," said the overseer. "When you are ready you can come out. Then you can tell me what you think."

The tiny door opened. Hare stepped inside.

"Just say 'I'm ready now' when you want to come out," said the voice.

The door closed behind her—and vanished.

Hare was standing on lush green grass in a buttercup-laden field. Tall oak and sycamore trees grew at one end; a hedge with a stile ran along the other. Along one side ran a small burbling river shaded with willow trees. Two horses galloped around the field, snorting, kicking their heels up, and occasionally nuzzling each other's necks. One was jet black with one white foot and a star on his forehead; the other was a tall chestnut mare with a long, handsome neck. Down her forehead was a white streak. They were so happy with each other that they took no notice of Hare.

On the other side of the field was a wooden fence and behind it a cottage with smoke spiraling lazily from a chimney. The garden around it was full of vegetables. Hare felt a tremor of fear at the thought that humans might live there. But it hardly lasted a second. The landscape she stood in seemed too good to be true—even up to the heather-covered hills that stretched away into the distance behind the house.

Suddenly, through the hedge scrambled a rabbit. He hopped cheekily up to Hare, who saw with some surprise that he wore a blue jacket with brass buttons.

"Hello," he said. "My name's Peter. What's yours?"

Before Hare could answer, Peter Rabbit was joined by three more rabbits. They did not wear human clothes; indeed one of them, with a big growth of fur on his head, looked as though he would make short work of anyone who tried to make him. With him was one much smaller rabbit and another who seemed to be the leader.

"Who are you?" said the leader, who had a limp.

"Hare," said Hare.

"Never heard of you," said the smallest new rabbit.

"My name is Hazel," said the leader. "This"—indicating the large, fierce, and fur-capped rabbit—"is Bigwig. The small one is Fiver."

Hare's head was spinning. Who were these animals? Why could she understand them so easily when her own kind couldn't make head or tail of her?

Rustling footsteps sounded in the grass behind her. She turned and saw a water rat and a mole coming toward her from the stream. A large toad bounded alongside, and waddling out from the trees to meet them was a badger. The four joined the group. The toad looked at Hare.

"I say," he said. "She's not from the Wild Wood, is she?"

"She looks much too nice for that," said the Water Rat.

"Now look here, hold on a minute, chaps," said the Mole. "Some of the Wild Wooders are jolly good sorts, you know."

Badger, all through this conversation, had been peering closely at Hare. At last he spoke.

"I knew her father," he said gruffly.

More animals arrived. Two dogs, a black mongrel and a smooth-haired, black-and-white fox terrier who had something wrong with the top of his head. A friendly, motherly hedgehog with an apron. A kitten called Tom, his mother Tabitha, and a villainous-looking rat called Samuel. Another cat, large and marmalade in color. A friendly pig called Wilbur—and some pig he was—with a family of spiders. Yet another pig who appeared to think he was a dog. A well-dressed mouse named Stuart. And even more; striding across the field came animals who must have walked a very long way indeed. A big brown bear. A leopard. A mongoose. And more, more, more. A humorous fox called Danny whom Hare felt she wouldn't trust an inch. Another fox, this one very sinister, called Mr. Tod. A parrot who kept on screaming "Pieces of eight" at her for no reason that she could fathom. And *all* of them could make themselves understood in that mysterious way she now seemed to have mastered for herself.

In the end their chattering turned into one overriding question.

"Why are you here?"

"I don't know," said Hare.

"You must," said Toad.

"We all know why we're here," said Hazel.

"I know why she's here," said Fiver suddenly. "She's a Queen."

First the overseer, now this rabbit. Why did they say such things to her?

"Don't you want to be here?" said Peter Rabbit.

Hare looked at them. She thought—*Yes, I do want to be here. I want to be with you all. I like you. I can talk to you. You can talk to me. For all the eternity of time left to me, it would be terrible to go to a place where I can talk to everyone but they can't talk to me.*

And then she thought again. *What right have I to be here? These animals know each other. They know what this place is and why they belong. I belong in the other place.*

Now she saw that the animals had formed a huge circle around her.

"Join us, Hare," they chanted. "We want you, Hare. You belong, Hare."

But I don't, she thought. *I would love to, but I don't. An* enormous sadness flooded through her. How she would love to stay forever. But she had no right, no right at all.

Then she remembered the instructions of the overseer.

"I am ready now," she said.

The open door appeared suddenly behind her. She turned and moved—slowly and with a feeling of great regret—through it. There was a click as the latch shut; she was standing alone once more on the golden platform in deep blue space.

"Well?" The overseer's voice again.

"What does it mean?" said Hare. "Who were those animals? What have I got to do with them?"

"Remember," said the overseer. "Think back. Recall what happened in your life."

Hare thought.

Life had gone on minute by minute. There was never any past or future; only the urge to survive the pinpoint of time that was the present. But now a long train of remembrance entered her mind. Being a leveret; taken by her mother to a separate form so she never knew brothers or sisters; starting her solitary life; mating; having her own leverets year after year; leaving each one in its separate place; feeding at night; the exhilaration of running, leaping, bounding; the terror of the hunt; the horror of the everlasting fight for survival. Then she recalled again the events of that last morning; the fight with the hawk; the final death dealt by the ominous red beast.

That was her life. That was what being a hare had meant.

The overseer waited patiently. Then the voice spoke again.

"Now think again."

Different visions came into Hare's mind—those same vivid pictures she had seen before, which meant nothing to her but were startlingly clear.

But what did they *mean*? Those things that had not happened. She *knew* they had not happened.

Yet she remembered them as though they had. She felt the danger of the hunt; heard huge machines more frightening than any red beast rumbling along behind her. She knew all the sensations of dodging frantically through a street crowded with humans. She was wearing a strange black garment and the body her mind was controlling was not a hare's. But she knew also a feeling of triumph as she eluded every attempt to catch her. And then she felt the warmth of a close friendship—a feeling completely new to her—with an old, soft-voiced, frail woman in black.

The overseer spoke.

"You are an animal just like all the others who have gone through the big door. You lived your life through and it came to an end. This happens to all the animals that have ever been. They live; they die; nobody knows; nobody cares. Who cries when a weasel dies? Who thinks twice when the life of a nuthatch comes to an end?"

"And who stops when a hare is run over?" said Hare.

"Exactly," said the overseer. "Only, this time people did care. And then they turned you into something special. They put you in a story."

"A what?" said Hare.

"Did you like the animals you met behind the small door?" asked the overseer.

"Yes," said Hare. "But I am not like them."

"You are," said the overseer. "Every animal you met there is in a story. The stories are all written now; they had their beginnings, their middles, and their ends, but now they are complete. That's where their lives are—in those stories. But those stories can happen again and those animals can have their lives over again every time a human sits down to read."

"Ah. Humans," said Hare.

"Yes. Humans," said the overseer. "They aren't entirely to

be feared or hated. They made up the stories and they repeat them. So the animals never die. Their heaven is here, a special one, close to but separate from the other animals."

"But I'm a *real* hare," said Hare. "I'm not in a story."

"Yes, you are," said the overseer. "You are in a story that meant a lot to the humans who made it up. You'll stay in their minds forever—but not as an ordinary hare bounding across the fields near their homes. No. You are the Queen of the Hares, savior of her people, who did great things."

Hare thought again. The memories of her hare life were strong. But so were the visions of her story-life; vivid and immediate like events that had only just happened.

"But those things aren't *true*. They never really happened to me." Hare's voice was full of anguish.

"As far as the children are concerned they happened. When you are remembered—as you will be in years to come—it will not be as a hare but as the great Queen of the Hares. This may not be true. But things are not untrue just because they never happened. In people's minds they are far more real. And the Queen of the Hares, whom the children thought about very deeply, is more real to them than Hare, whom they never knew until she was dead."

Hare was silent.

"Come now, Hare," said the overseer gently. "It is time to make your choice."

Hare sighed. She wanted to join the little band of happy talking creatures in their perfect, sun-filled landscape.

Then she thought again of the great tide of fur, feather, and scale pouring through the golden door. They didn't have the power of language, of thought, of understanding, beyond their own furious struggles to stay alive. All they could really gain in this new place was absence of fear.

But they were her kind; she was one of them. If she really was a Queen, then she was *their* Queen.

The choice was before her. Story or truth? Temptation or duty? What she would like or what she thought she ought to do?

"Well?" said the overseer. "Have you made up your mind?"

"No," cried Hare. "I can't choose."

Children

Kirsty's mother volunteered to type the story. She used her new electronic daisy-wheel machine and the result was beautiful. When the children saw the master copies before Mr. Bray took them to the Teachers' Center along with his introduction telling how the story came to be written, they gasped with surprise and awe. Their words looked unreal, transfigured—completely removed from those they had written and spoken. But when they looked again they saw that there was no doubt about it—they were definitely the very same words.

Already a fair-copied and illustrated version was displayed all around the room. Each child had also done a careful picture to be printed in the book with his or her own part of the story.

Harry made the wooden gravestone he had promised. He chiseled RIP THE QUEEN OF THE HARES onto a two-inch-thick offcut from a felled tree trunk. He had dipped it in creosote, applied a coat of exterior Ronseal, and then screwed two metal strips to the back extending downward a foot so it would stay firmly in the ground.

Then school returned to normal. Three weeks later the bound copies arrived from the Teachers' Center. The children seized them eagerly. The pink card covers were smartly printed in Letraset:

THE QUEEN OF THE HARES

Underneath were the names of everybody in the class. The black spiral binding looked very smart and there were more gasps—this time of pleasure—when the children opened their copies.

"It's a real book," said Sarah.

"It *is* a real book," said Mr. Bray. "It's on sale at the Teachers' Center. And in the bookshop in town. People are *buying* it."

"With real money?" asked Tim. "Will we get any?"

"I fear not," said Mr. Bray. "It's just a pathetic attempt to cover the costs."

Everyone who contributed to the story was given a free copy. At the end of the day, Sarah and Harry walked home carrying theirs very carefully. They passed the church, the village post office and shop, and the new houses on the edge of the village. Then they headed out up the open road toward Spinney Farm, ambling contentedly along the grassy shoulder.

After twenty minutes or so they stopped.

"This is where we found Hare," said Sarah.

"Isn't it strange," said Harry. "We carried her into school and now we're carrying her out of school again. In a sort of way."

He looked at his copy of the book.

"I wonder where she came from," said Sarah.

Harry looked toward the grove at the summit of the down.

"Up there," he said. "There's lots of things hiding in the wood and around it. Hares among them."

"Let's go up there and have a look," said Sarah.

The sun on this hot June afternoon warmed their backs as they walked up the shallow grassy rise. Fifty yards from

the grove they stood and looked back. The view was a wide one. Below, the road stretched like a dark gray ribbon into the village. As they watched, the bus bringing the secondary-school children home from the town passed along it. Far over to the right, on the other side of the road, they could see their own farmhouse and all its familiar surrounding outbuildings. Beyond that the patchwork landscape stretched into the distance. Far away was the straight gash of the highway; even at this distance they could hear a faint roar from its traffic.

"Let's sit down," said Sarah.

"Isn't the grass short here," said Harry.

Sarah had a sudden idea.

"I bet this is where the hares eat," she said. "I bet she was eating here before she ran down to the road."

"Could be," said Harry. "But why should she take it into her head to run all that way?"

"Mr. Bray said they just like running. Besides, the Queen of the Hares ran for miles and miles," said Sarah.

"She had a purpose," said Harry. "Anyway, that's just a story."

"It's not *just* a story," said Sarah, hugging the book to her knees. "It's *our* story. It's *her* story."

Harry was looking upward.

"See up there," he said, pointing. "There's a hawk, hovering."

Sarah looked where he was pointing. A small object hung in the sky. It looked menacing even at that distance.

"I'd love to know why Hare ran all the way down to the road," said Harry. "And how she got those scratches on her."

"It couldn't be barbed wire, that's for sure," said Sarah.

Suddenly the hawk was gone.

"Some poor creature's been caught," said Harry.

"Let's go home," said Sarah. "That's upset me a bit."

"*Look!*" said Harry suddenly, and gripped Sarah's arm tightly.

Below them, about sixty yards away, a brown animal with long ears ran purposefully.

"It's a hare," Sarah and Harry shouted together.

The hare was coming uphill at an angle across their line of vision. They saw its great bounding strides and even from so far away could feel the strength of those huge hind legs.

The hare stopped, thirty yards away from them. It rose on its hind legs and looked fearlessly at Sarah and Harry. Its ears and whiskers twitched as if in greeting; then it was gone, racing past them and around the side of the grove until it was lost from view.

"Marvelous," said Harry. "It was just like Hare. The white tummy and golden-brown legs. And couldn't it *go!*"

He turned to Sarah—and saw, to his surprise, that she was crying.

"Poor Hare." She sniffed. "She should still be here. This is where she lived all her life. I bet she loved it up here on the hill with the others."

"She's still here," said Harry. "She'll always be here. To us, at any rate. But"—and he patted his copy of the book— "she's in here as well."

Brother and sister stood silently together. They both shared the same thought. They saw in their minds a strong, brown, streamlined creature leaping and running silently across the downs forever. Sometimes the creature was just a hare going about her hare's business. Sometimes there was a crown on her head and she was weighed down with great responsibilities. But still she ran across the grass and woodland of her home and soon Harry and Sarah realized that they could tell no difference between the hare who lived on the downs and the great Queen of the Hares herself.

"Come on," said Sarah at last. "They'll be worried about us at home if we stay out any longer."

S I X

Decision

Hare did not move. She was listening to messages that came from impossibly far away. She knew the overseer waited patiently for her decision.

And now she saw two children sitting where once she had sat—on her last morning, feeding at dawn. She heard their words and understood them. And the words helped her.

If she went with the other animals she would still go as Queen. She remembered how she had, on her journey to this place, felt sorry and responsible for them; the same feeling that she had in the story toward the creatures in the valley. Besides, were she to go with the great mass, she would not pass into oblivion. She would be remembered. Sarah had said so.

But what about the other place? She was fit to go there too. She knew that now. She lived in a story that children had made and would give to their children. She would always be Queen of the Hares and always, for somebody, be doing great deeds. So wherever she went, she was fit. She was wanted.

At last she was ready to speak to the overseer.

"I have made up my mind," she said. "I know now which door I want to go through."

AUTHOR'S NOTE

Two people I respect immensely gave me great, although at the time unwitting, help in the writing of this story. One is Mr. Donald Fisher, County Education Officer for Hertfordshire, who at a time when I was very ill gave me a wonderful book which helped me get better and started me thinking. It was *The Leaping Hare* by George Ewart Evans and David Thomson (also author of *Danny Fox*, best of all animal characters). The other is Mr. John Emanuel, Headmaster of High Wych JMI School in Hertfordshire, who in recounting experiences in the classroom told of an event in his school which provided the beginnings of another of this story's main elements. Another person I admired immensely but certainly never met was E. M. Forster, one of the greatest writers of the century. I give him more generalized thanks for his marvelous short story "The Celestial Omnibus," which has haunted me for more years than I care to remember. Finally, I am deeply indebted to Mr. Richard Adams, who not only let me use and put words into the mouths of some of his characters but also made valuable suggestions as to how they might best be presented.